KT-115-821

Copyright © 2022

make believe ideas ltd

The Wilderness, Berkhamsted, Hertfordshire, HP4 2AZ, UK.
6th Floor, South Bank House, Barrow Street, Dublin 4, D04 TR29, Ireland.

www.makebelieveideas.co.uk

Written by Patch Moore.
Illustrated by Clare Fennell.

Inspired by the American folk song, 'We're Going on a Bear Hunt!'

This book belongs to

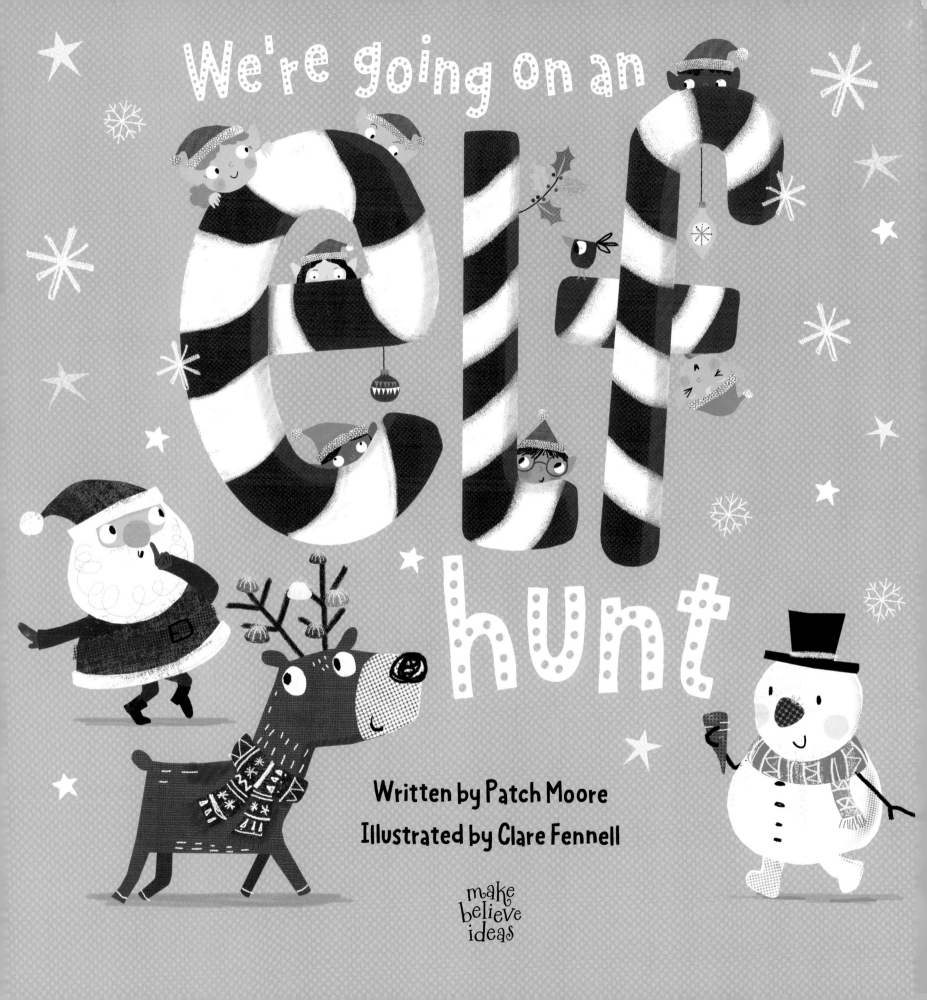

We're going on an Elf hunt

Written by Patch Moore

Illustrated by Clare Fennell

make believe ideas

We're going on an

ELF

hunt.

We're going to **find** some **helpers**.

It's nearly Christmas.

We're not **worried!**

PRESENT FACTORY

ON   OFF

BACK SOON!

What's this?

A **forest!** A candy cane forest.

We can't go **around** it.

We can't go **over** it.

Jingle bells!

We've got to go **through** it.

Let's go . . . ho-ho-ho!
Crunch! Munch!
CRUNCH! MUNCH!
Who's there?

An elf!

We're going on an **elf hunt.**

We're going to **find** some **helpers.**

A **river!** A merry berry river.

We can't go **around** it.

We can't go **over** it.

Jingle bells!

We've got to go **across** it.

Let's go . . . **ho-ho-ho!**

Splash! Slurp!
SPLOSH! BURP!
Who's there?

An **elf!**

We're going on an **elf hunt.**

We're going to **find** some **helpers.**

It's nearly **Christmas.** We're not **worried!**

What's this?

A **mountain!** A marshmallow mountain.
We can't go **around** it.
We can't go **under** it.
Jingle bells!
We've got to climb **over** it.

Let's go ... **ho-ho-ho!**
Wibble! **Nibble!**
WIBBLE! NIBBLE!
Who's there?

An **elf!**

We're going on an **elf** hunt.

We're going to **find** some **helpers**.

A **house?** A gingerbread house.

Ho-ho-ho!

It's **busy** in here.

So many **toys.**

Lots of **Christmas cheer.**

And . . .

all the **ELVES!**

Out of the gingerbread house.

Don't forget the **toys!**

Back **over** the marshmallow mountain.
Wibble! Nibble!

Back across the merry berry river.
Splash! Splosh!

Back through the candy cane forest.
Munch! Crunch!

Back to the **sleigh.** Ready to go.

It's nearly **Christmas.**

Ho-ho-ho!

We're going on a **present hunt.**
We're going to find the **best** one.
It's finally

Christmas.

We're so

EXCITED!